MOLLY BANG

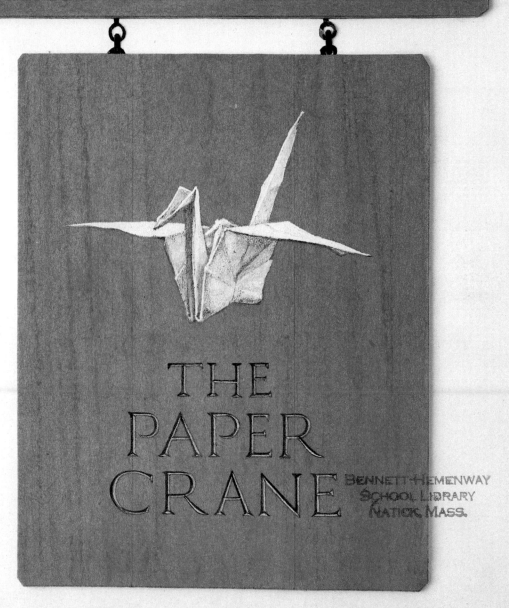

THE
PAPER
CRANE

GREENWILLOW BOOKS, NEW YORK

Library of Congress Cataloging in Publication Data

Bang, Molly.   The paper crane.
    Summary: A mysterious man enters a restaurant and pays for his
dinner with a paper crane that magically comes alive and dances.
    1. Children's stories, American.   [1. Cranes (Birds)—Fiction]
I. Title.   PZ7.B2217Pap 1985   [E]   84-13546
ISBN 0-688-04108-6   ISBN 0-688-04109-4 (lib. bdg.)

The full-color art, paper cutouts, was
photographed by Ned Manter to retain the
three-dimensional quality of the originals.

To Libby, Ava, and Susan
with much love and thanks
for all these years

Special thanks to Jelle Atema
and his flute,
to Dick and Monika,
and to Carol Reinisch

A man once owned a restaurant on a busy road.
He loved to cook good food and he loved to serve it.
He worked from morning until night, and he was happy.

But a new highway was built close by. Travelers drove straight from one place to another and no longer stopped at the restaurant. Many days went by when no guests came at all. The man became very poor, and had nothing to do but dust and polish his empty plates and tables.

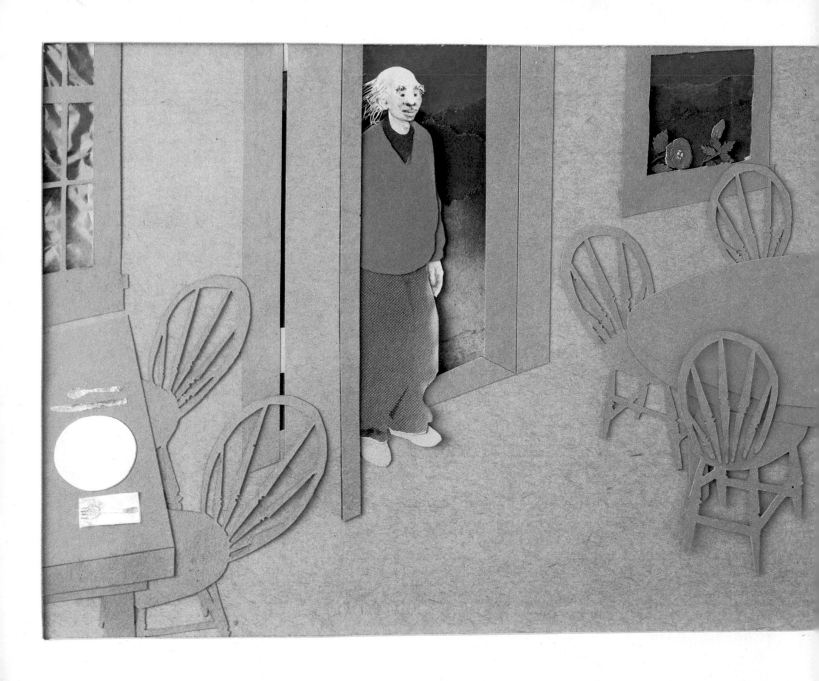

One evening a stranger came into the restaurant. His clothes were old and worn, but he had an unusual, gentle manner.

Though he said he had no money to pay for food, the owner invited him to sit down. He cooked the best meal he could make and served him like a king.

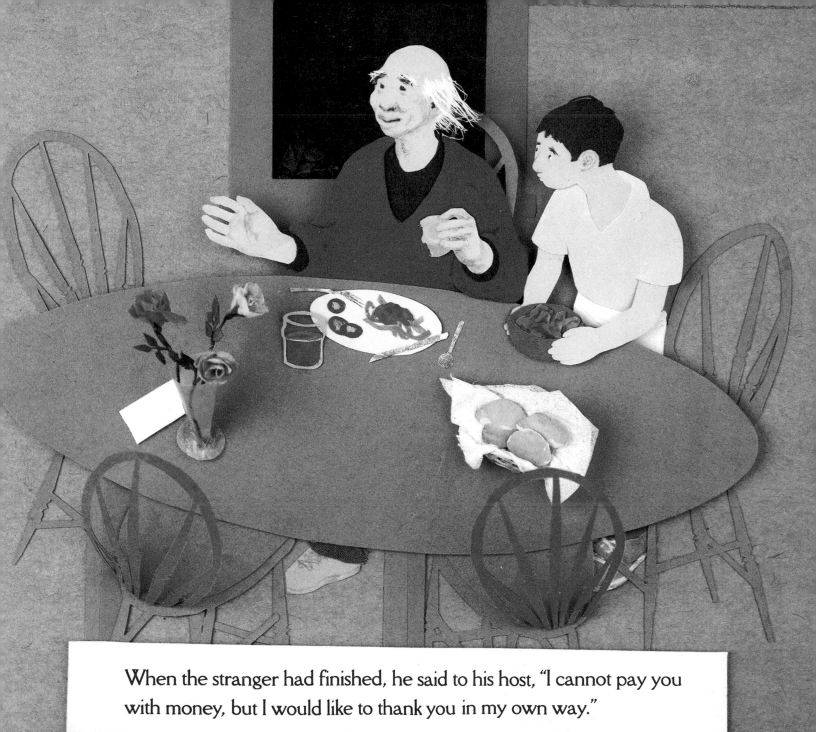

When the stranger had finished, he said to his host, "I cannot pay you with money, but I would like to thank you in my own way."

He picked up a paper napkin from the table and folded
it into the shape of a crane. "You have only to clap your
hands," he said, "and this bird will come to life and dance
for you. Take it, and enjoy it while it is with you."
With these words the stranger left.

It happened just as the stranger had said. The owner had only to clap his hands and the paper crane became a living bird, flew down to the floor, and danced.

Soon word of the dancing crane spread, and people came
from far and near to see the magic bird perform.

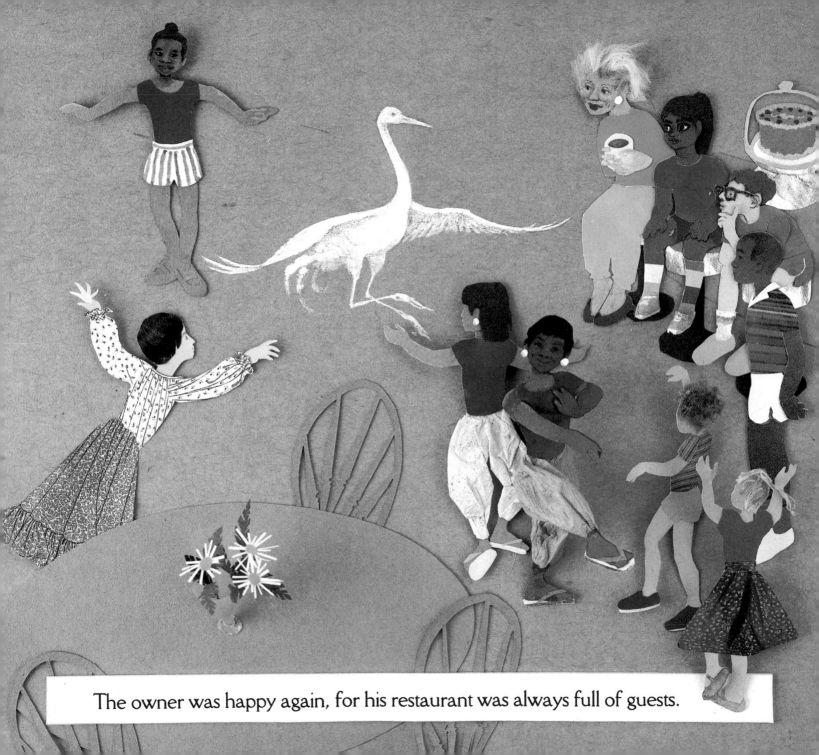

The owner was happy again, for his restaurant was always full of guests.

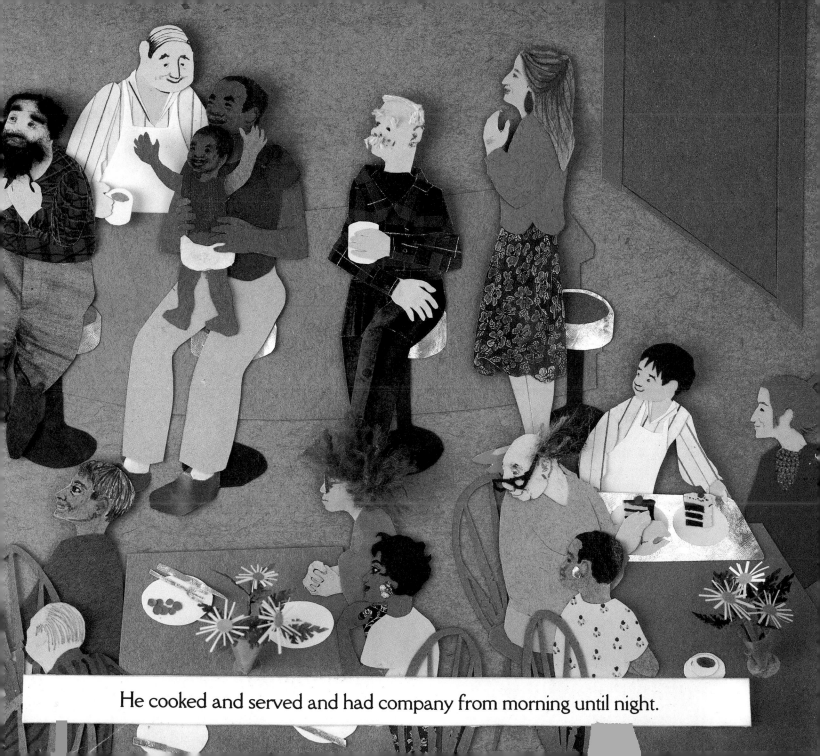

He cooked and served and had company from morning until night.

The weeks passed.

And the months.

One evening a man came into the restaurant. His clothes were old and worn, but he had an unusual, gentle manner. The owner knew him at once and was overjoyed.

The stranger, however, said nothing. He took a flute from his pocket, raised it to his lips, and began to play.

The crane flew down from its place on the shelf
and danced as it had never danced before.

The stranger finished playing, lowered the flute from his lips,
and returned it to his pocket. He climbed on the back
of the crane, and they flew out of the door and away.

The restaurant still stands by the side of the road, and guests still come to eat the good food and hear the story of the gentle stranger and the magic crane made from a paper napkin. But neither the stranger nor the dancing crane has ever been seen again.

Bang, Molly

The paper crane

DATE DUE		
'MAY JAN 1 9 '95		
JAN 1 1 FEB 2 1 '96		
SEP 2 7		
OCT 2 7 '89 NOV 03 2000		
DEC 9 1993 MAR X 1 2002		
JAN 4 '94 OCT 2 4 2006		
MAR 1 5 1994		
APR 6 1994		
APR 1 6 1994		
APR 1 3 1994		
NOV. 1 4 1995		